All Aboard the
DINOTRAIN

DEB LUND

Illustrated by

HOWARD FINE

Requests for permission to make copies of any part of the work
should be mailed to the following address: Permissions Department, Harcourt, Inc.,
6277 Sea Harbor Drive, Orlando, Florida 32887-6777.

www.HarcourtBooks.com

Library of Congress Cataloging-in-Publication Data
Lund, Deb.
All aboard the dinotrain/Deb Lund; illustrated by Howard Fine.
p.   cm.
Summary: When dinosaurs seek adventure by taking a train ride,
they find the trip has some unexpected surprises along the way.
[1. Dinosaurs—Fiction. 2. Railroads—Trains—Fiction. 3. Travel—Fiction. 4. Stories in rhyme.]
I. Fine, Howard, 1961- ill. II. Title.
PZ8.3.L9715Al 2006
[E]—dc22   2004019108
ISBN-13: 978-0152-05237-9   ISBN-10: 0-15-205237-2

First edition
A C E G H F D B

Printed in Singapore

The illustrations in this book were done in gouache and watercolors.
The display type was set in Opti Morgan Three and rendered on the cover by Howard Fine.
The text type was set in Barcelona Bold.
Color separations by Colourscan Co. Pte. Ltd., Singapore
Printed and bound by Tien Wah Press, Singapore
This book was printed on totally chlorine-free Stora Enso Matte paper.
Production supervision by Ginger Boyer
Designed by Linda Lockowitz

For Michael
—D. L.

For Michael, Andrea, Yogi, and Boo-Boo
—H. F.

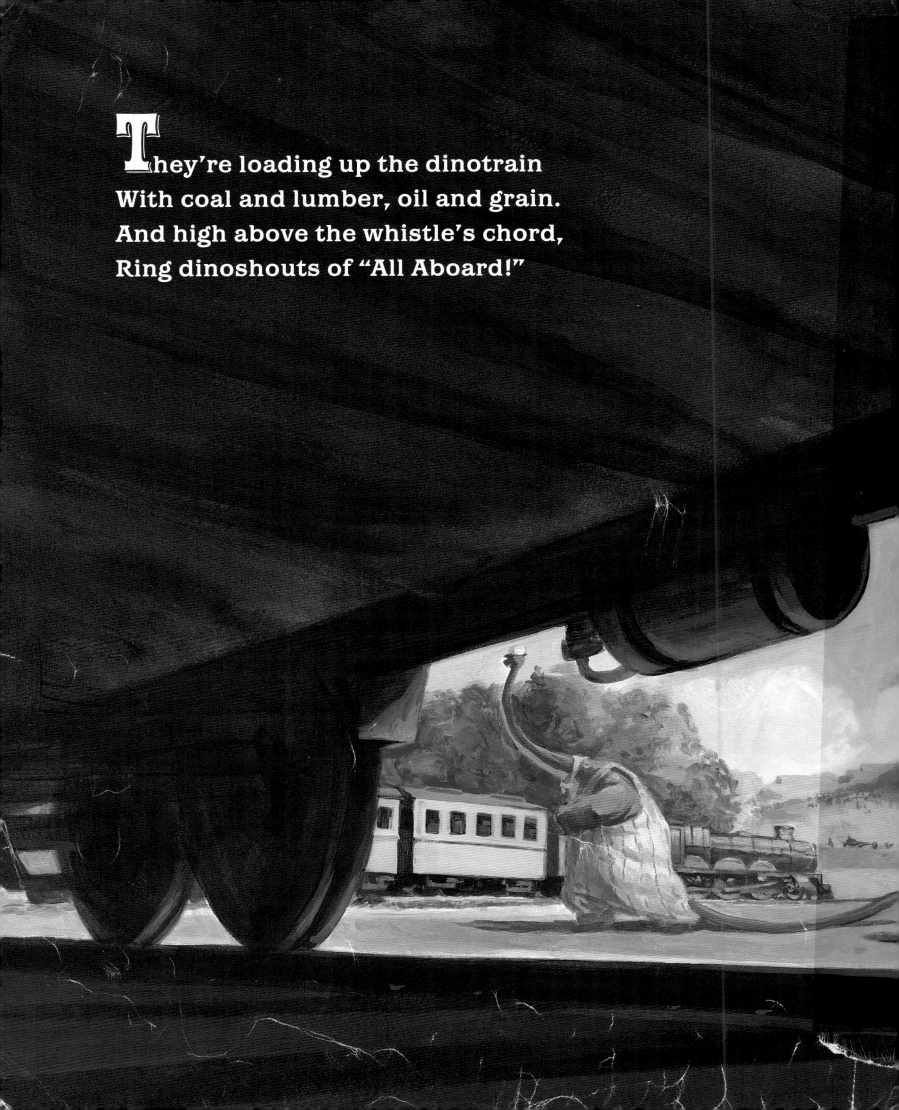

They're loading up the dinotrain
With coal and lumber, oil and grain.
And high above the whistle's chord,
Ring dinoshouts of "All Aboard!"

The dinostoker shovels coal.
The flames are under his control.
The dinoboiler builds up steam.
Soon pistons pump a rhythmic theme.

"Farewell!" the dinofamilies cry.
With cheers, the dinos wave good-bye.
Adventures wait just down the track.
"We're off!" they say. "But we'll be back!"

The engine coughs and dinochugs.
The train moves like a line of slugs.
"We haven't traveled very far.
Let's dinopush each railroad car!"

"We think we can!" they dinosay.
"Our dinomight will save the day."
The smokestack coughs out dinosoot.
They sweat from dinohead to foot.

The hill's too steep for that much weight,
And so they toss the dinofreight.
Without a load, they quickly climb
And reach the peak in dinotime.

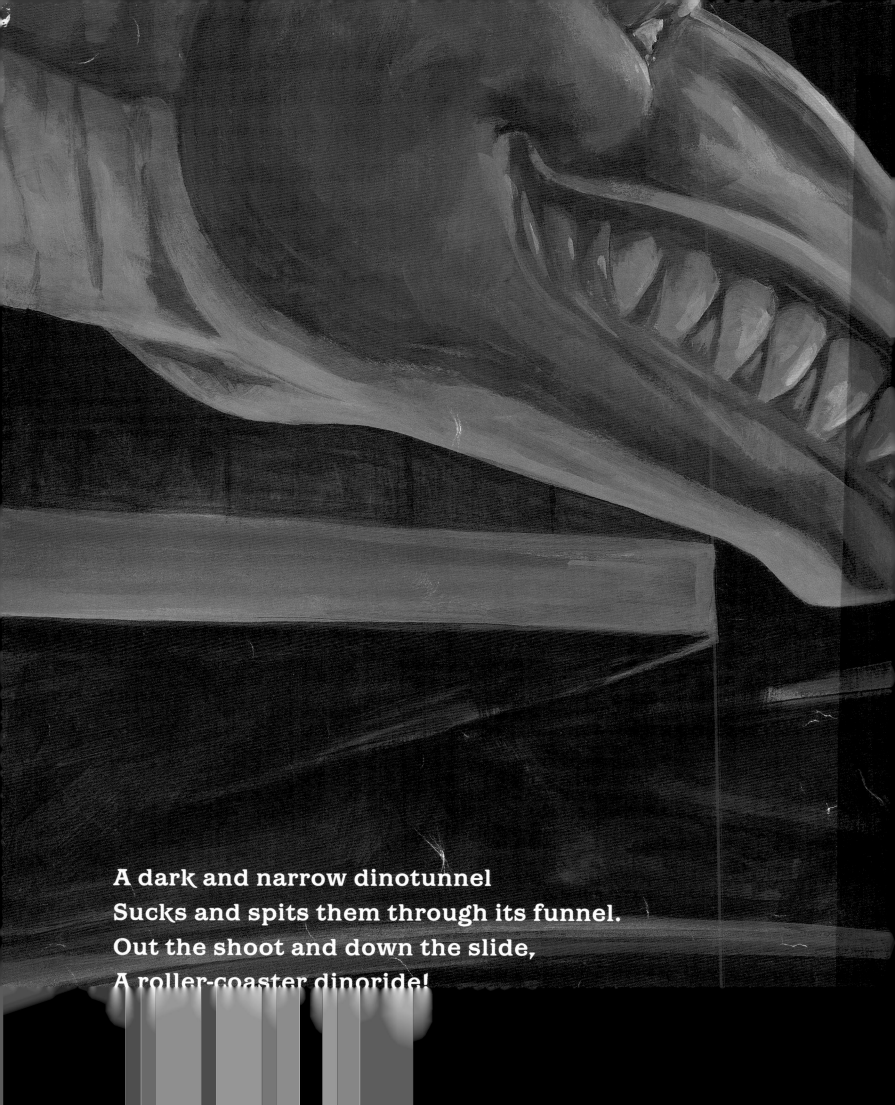

A dark and narrow dinotunnel
Sucks and spits them through its funnel.
Out the shoot and down the slide,
A roller-coaster dinoride!

They dinoscream and squeal, "Yippee!"
And wave their dinoarms with glee.
When the cars tip left or right,
They lean way out and hang on tight.

"Oh no!" the dinobrakemen shout.
"The train won't stop. The trestle's out!"
And as the bridge is growing near,
Their joy turns into dinofear.

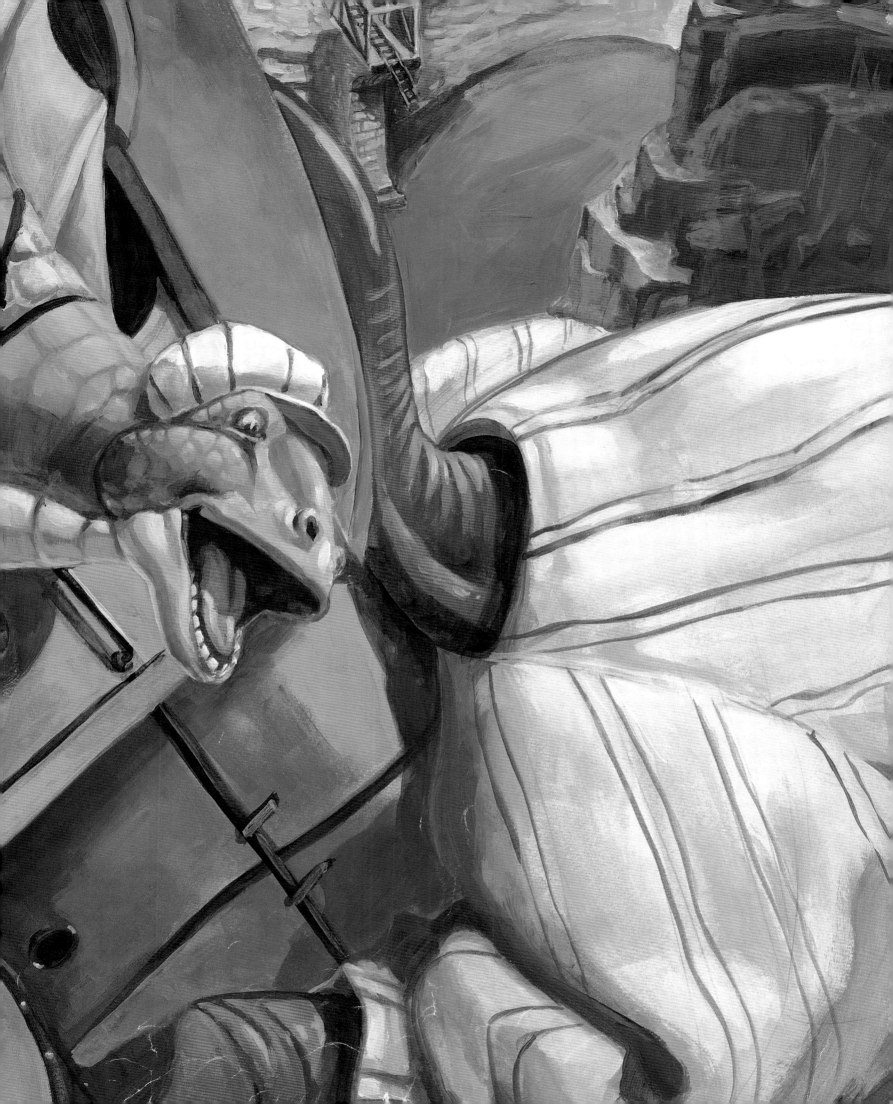

They clamber up and cling on top,
Unsure of how they'll dinostop.
They dinoduck and hide their eyes,
But then they get a *big* surprise.

They dinorocket off the bridge,
While train cars fly from ridge to ridge.
The train goes on without a crash.
"We're dinoflying!" Then . . .

They dinogroan, "How can it be?
We thought this trip was water-free!
What made us want to dinoroam?
Let's shake this lake and head back home!"

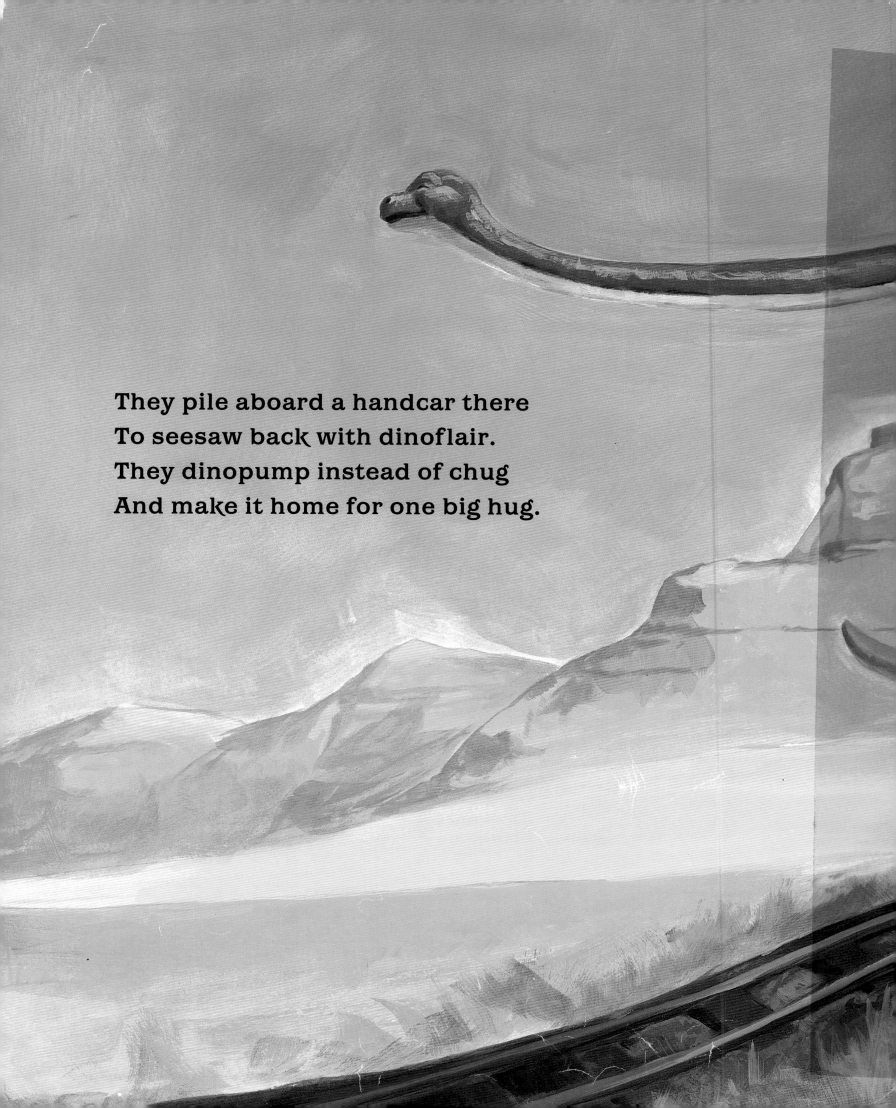

They pile aboard a handcar there
To seesaw back with dinoflair.
They dinopump instead of chug
And make it home for one big hug.

Though dinotight in that embrace,
They still find dinodreams to chase.
"We'll *never* take another train . . .

But how about a dino*plane*?"

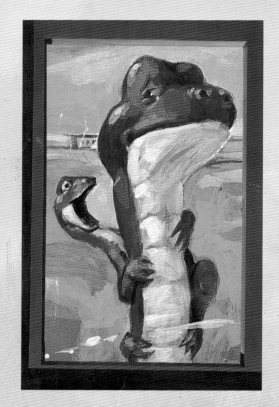

ENGINEER
Brachiosaurus
(with assistant)

BRAKE OPERATOR
Spinosaurus

SWITCH OPERATOR
Triceratops

Your

D   I   N